Best Friends
Together Again

by
ALIKI

 Greenwillow Books, New York

Watercolor paints, colored pencils, and a black pen were used for the full-color art. The text type is Helvetica. Copyright © 1995 by Aliki Brandenberg. All rights reserved. No part of this book may be reproduced or utilized in any form or by any means, electronic or mechanical, including photocopying, recording, or by any information storage and retrieval system, without permission in writing from the Publisher, Greenwillow Books, a division of William Morrow & Company, Inc., 1350 Avenue of the Americas, New York, NY 10019.
Printed in Hong Kong by Wing King Tong.   First Edition   10 9 8 7 6 5 4 3 2 1

Library of Congress Cataloging-in-Publication Data:
Aliki.   Best friends together again / by Aliki.   p.   cm.   Summary: When Robert's best friend Peter, who moved away, comes back to visit, various emotions surface, but mostly pleasure—which all the old friends share.   ISBN 0-688-13753-9 (trade).   ISBN 0-688-13754-7 (lib. bdg.)
[1. Friendship—Fiction. 2. Moving, Household—Fiction.]   I. Title.   PZ7.A397Be   1995   [E]—dc20   94-12989   CIP   AC

*Here's
to
family, friends,
and
reunions*

This was the day.

Peter was coming!

Robert had read Peter's letter so many times,
it was crumpled and worn.

Robert couldn't wait, either.

Ever since Peter had moved away,

Robert had missed him.

But now Robert's heart thumped.

Will Peter be the same? he wondered.

Will he still like me?

The doorbell rang.

"Hello, Peter," said Robert.

Something is different, thought Robert.

I forgot he had curly hair.

"Hello, Robert," said Peter.

Something is different, thought Peter.

That's not the nose I remember.

But Sparky was licking Peter, and they forgot
about what they had not remembered.
"Hey, Sparky," Peter said. "You're bigger,
but you're the same old Sparky."
Robert laughed.
"Just like us," he said.

"I brought you a surprise," said Peter.

"I made it myself."

"Oh, thank you! And it works," said Robert,

  as the paper airplane sailed through the hall.

They went into Robert's room.

"Your bed is turned around," said Peter.

"You have a new lamp. And lots more books."

"This is Moonface that I wrote to you about,"
 said Robert. He gave her to Peter to hold.

"She is soft as fluff," said Peter.

"I'll call her Fluffy Moonface."

"You could always think of good names,"
 said Robert.

Peter walked around the room.

"I remember the old toy chest," he said.

"And here are the puppets and the cars

and the blocks, just where they always were."

Robert and Peter built a fort, like old times.

"Remember that great tower we made,
 with all those ramps and people
 and cars?" asked Peter.

"Your mother took a photo and sent it
 to a magazine!"

"And we won second prize!" said Robert.

"I build with my new friend Alex," said Peter.

"But not like this."

"You wrote that Alex taught you to skate,"
 said Robert.

"Yes," said Peter. "And he taught me
 to make paper airplanes, too."

It was lunchtime.

"Your favorite sandwich
was peanut butter and jelly,"
said Robert.

"Yours was peanut butter
without jelly," said Peter.

And that is what they ate.

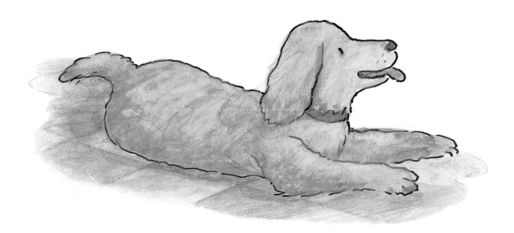

In the garden Robert said,

"You missed the tadpoles."

"But maybe we can find some frogs,"
said Peter.

"My friend Will knows all about frogs
and toads—where they live,
how they hibernate," said Robert.

"He wants to meet you."

Peter had heard all about Will,

but he wasn't sure he wanted to meet him.

"Is Will your best friend?" he asked.

"Will is just like a best friend," said Robert.

"You'll see. But he's not an oldest best friend, like us."

Will was there before they knew it.

"It must be great to be back," he told Peter.

"Look what Peter made," said Robert.

"His friend taught him."

"Awesome!" said Will.

The airplane landed under the couch.

"It needs wide-open spaces," said Robert.

"Let's go fly it in the park."

They ran across the path.

"Peter!" called a voice.

"It's Peter!" said another voice, and another.

"Peter's back!"

"Hi, Lee Ann. Hi, Ellie."

Peter's friends surrounded him.

They were as happy as only old friends can be.

"What a reunion!" said Ellie.

The friends tossed the airplane back and forth.

"I'd like to learn to make one, too," said Will.

"Me, too!" said Molly.

"Me, too! Me, too!" they all shouted.

"I can show you how," said Peter.

"Let's meet at my house tomorrow," said Will.

"We'll have a paper-folding party."

"And another reunion," said Ellie.

The next day the friends met.

They had juice. They had cookies.

And they folded paper into airplanes.

Then they went to the park to fly them.

Every day while Peter was there,
the friends got together to play.

But all too soon it was time to part.
"It will be great when you come
to visit me," said Peter.
"A visit is fun to look foward to,"
said Robert.
"And fun to remember," said Peter.
"Just like friends."